W9-CPE-322

A PERCY THE PARK KEEPER BOOK

1 2 3

NICK BUTTERWORTH

HarperCollins *Children's Books*

1 One

One wheelbarrow being
pushed by Percy the park keeper.

2 Two

Two boots. Percy makes sure
no one's hiding inside them!

3 Three

Three rabbits

hopping in the grass.

4 Four

Four cherry cupcakes

on the fox's imaginary tree. Yum!

5 Five

Five apples. It looks
like the hedgehog needs
Percy's help!

6 Six

Six mice going round and round. *Whee!*

7 Seven

Seven balloons floating by.
Percy hopes there's a party!

8 Eight

Eight friends having fun in the playground.

9 Nine

Nine watering cans

from Percy's collection.

A perfect place to hide!

10 Ten

Ten fingers wiggling in the air.
Settle down, everyone!

Counting is fun!

1 One mug

2 Two balloons

3 Three mice

4 Four pots

5 Five pegs

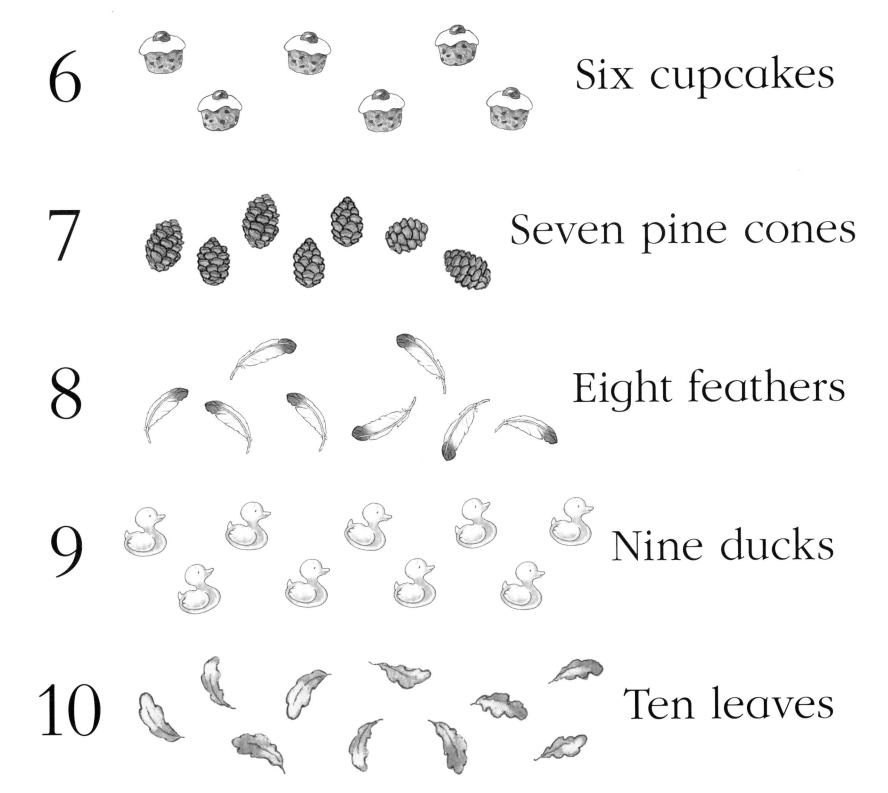

6   Six cupcakes

7   Seven pine cones

8   Eight feathers

9   Nine ducks

10   Ten leaves

First published in paperback in Great Britain by HarperCollins *Children's Books* in 2021

1 3 5 7 9 10 8 6 4 2

ISBN: 978-0-00-845194-3

HarperCollins *Children's Books* is a division of HarperCollins*Publishers* Ltd.
1 London Bridge Street, London SE1 9GF

www.harpercollins.co.uk

HarperCollins*Publishers*
1st Floor, Watermarque Building, Ringsend Road, Dublin 4, Ireland

Text copyright © Nick Butterworth 2021
Illustrations copyright © Nick Butterworth 1989, 1992, 1993, 1996, 1997, 1999, 2001, 2019, 2021

Nick Butterworth asserts the moral right to be identified as the author/illustrator of the work.
A CIP catalogue record for this title is available from the British Library. All rights reserved. No part of this
publication may be reproduced, stored in a retrieval system or transmitted in any form or by any means, electronic,
mechanical, photocopying, recording or otherwise, without the prior permission of HarperCollins*Publishers* Ltd.

Printed in Italy